Frances Anne Trevelyan

Quarr Abbey

Or the Mistaken Calling - A Tale of the Isle of Wight in the XIIIth Century

Frances Anne Trevelyan

Quarr Abbey
Or the Mistaken Calling - A Tale of the Isle of Wight in the XIIIth Century

ISBN/EAN: 9783337080112

Printed in Europe, USA, Canada, Australia, Japan

Cover: Foto ©Andreas Hilbeck / pixelio.de

More available books at **www.hansebooks.com**

Quarr Abbey,

OR,

THE MISTAKEN CALLING:

A TALE OF THE ISLE OF WIGHT IN THE XIIITH CENTURY.

BY

Frances A. Trevelyan,

AUTHOR OF LECTURES ON ENGLISH HISTORY.

LONDON:

RIVINGTONS, WATERLOO PLACE.

OXFORD: W. R. BOWDEN; RYDE: GIBBS, WAGNER, UNION-STREET.

1862.

TO

Miss Bowreman,

THE LAST OF HER NAME,

A NAME WHOSE MEMORY, LIKE THAT OF THE ABBOTS OF QUARR, IS

FAST FADING FROM THE SUNNY ISLAND WHERE BOTH WERE ONCE

FAMILIAR AS HOUSEHOLD WORDS,

BUT WHICH YET LIVES

IN THE AFFECTIONS OF NOT A FEW,

THIS LITTLE ATTEMPT TO RECAL THE FORGOTTEN PAST

IS,

WITH TRUE REGARD,

DEDICATED BY HER SINCERE FRIEND,

The Author.

OXFORD:
PRINTED BY W. R. BOWDEN,
HOLYWELL-STREET.

CONTENTS.

Preface.

A S the Abbot of Quarr may appear to the reader to be a mythical personage, a sort of "lusus naturæ," of whose existence reasonable doubts can be entertained, it is as well to state that he is in some sense a historical reality. But not, it may be argued, historical in the sense of the poem; since instead of the beautiful character there described, he was a haughty, imperious churchman, and his quarrel with Isabella de Fortibus nothing more nor less than an ambitious struggle for the patronage of livings to which, as sovereign of the Isle of Wight, she had clearly the right of presentation. But was the right so clear? On this point a doubt may fairly be surmised. There are two sides to most questions; and it is more than probable that an excellent case might be made out for the Abbot of Quarr had we but access to the documents of the period. Nevertheless, as this is neither the place nor the moment for controversial discussion, a single fact in the Abbot's favour is all that shall now be adduced. It is this:—that when the noble lady to whom allusion has been made, lay upon her death-bed, although two Bishops were in attendance upon her, she could not die in peace until the Abbot of Quarr had been duly summoned. She was at this time far away from the Isle of Wight. But it was her wish, nay, her injunction, that he should be sent for; and her wish was obeyed, and he arrived in time to close her eyes.

Surely such a desire, expressed at such a moment, looks like a belief in his sanctity. Let it stand, however, for as much as it is worth, and no more; for scarcely any particulars of the Abbey history are now extant. Ruthlessly destroyed by Henry VIII., almost razed to the ground, its records have disappeared. Not even a catalogue of its Abbots remains. There was a Stephen of Lexington among the number, famed for holiness of life and manners: he was a disciple of S. Edmund of Canterbury. There was an Andrew, (possibly our Abbot,) and afterwards a

Thomas, who lived in the reign of Edward IV., and whose name occurs upon an ancient deed to which the seal of his Abbey is appended; but little more can be authenticated. The waves of time, more relentless than those that lash the adjacent coast, have swept away its fair proportions, its walls are mostly removed or reconstructed, the quarries are no longer worked, the woods are felled.

Just enough of the ruin remains, just enough of its history can be revived, to invest the deserted precincts with a more than ideal interest. And those, who, with the writer, have felt that such memories are good, and that their influence, rightly received, is improving; as leading us to emulate, if not the actual regulations of past institutions, the piety and self-sacrifice of many amongst their founders and occupants, will scarcely deem that the tale has been written in vain. Its publication, however, at the present time, has other than an ethical object. Originally written merely as the recreation of a passing hour, it is now printed to aid the funds of a school in which the writer is deeply interested, as supplying what is much wanted in the present day—a home where young girls are protected during the dangerous interval between leaving the National Schools and entering respectable service, and where they likewise receive elementary instruction in the duties of their future calling.

Such institutions are humble attempts to combine the spirit of the past with the utilitarian views of the nineteenth century; and the object being one with which most persons can sympathize, it is hoped that it will plead in behalf of the poem more eloquently than any intrinsic merit which may seem to be assumed by its publication.

And with this hope the writer bids each kind and sympathizing reader a hearty " FAREWELL !"

The profits of this little publication will be given in aid of the funds of St. Michael's School for Training Servants, Wantage, Berks.

INTRODUCTION.

A few rude foot-prints of far-off times,
Set in a frame of homely rhymes.
Exhumed sub-strata, and fossil remains,
From the "Garden Isle," and her sea-girt plains.
Primary rock from the Abbey walls;
   And moss from its ruins that prostrate lie;
Reader, my tale for forbearance calls :—
   Who knock about stones, hit the passers by !

QUARR ABBEY:

&c.

PART I.

𝔗𝔥𝔢 𝔄𝔟𝔟𝔬𝔱.

I.

"So, separate from the world, his breast
Might duly take, and strongly keep
The print of Heaven."

Keble's Christian Year.

HE Knight, he threw his armour down,
 And he turned his back on tower and town,
 And he told his beads as he rode along,
For his heart was weary of slight and wrong.
"He would fain to the Abbey," he said, "repair,
To end his days in repose and prayer."
And when he came to the Abbey gate
He had but a little time to wait ;

The coming was quickly noised abroad,
Of the mighty man, with the mighty sword,
Who had vowed to lay down his earthly cares,
And give to the Church his wealth and prayers.
Very happy he felt that day;
Though he fell asleep when he meant to pray!

II.

But time went on, and the Knight 'professed,'
With his hands laid meekly across his breast :—
And glad were the brethren all to see
His air of deep humility.
And humble he meant to be, no doubt,
Though *how* he had not yet found out.
"You must part with your horse and hound, 'tis plain,
Sir Knight," said the Abbot frank;
" They will win back your thoughts to earth again,
And remind you of your rank."
The Knight loved to look on a holy look,
And a spare ascetic frame,
Much self-denial himself could brook,

And could stand some words of blame;
But a thrust that came home in such very plain form
Stirred his very hot temper quite into a storm!
" What?" said he, and he stamped his foot
As he'd stamped in days of yore,
Forgetting that now he had never a boot
'Twixt his skin and the hard stone floor.
What? shall he " must his must" to me,
As if I his serf had come to be!
Surely my good old steed might range
For the rest of his days in the Abbey Grange.
Hundreds of acres I gave by deed
To enlarge his Abbey's bound;
How dares he grudge my good horse a feed?
Or to kennel my noble hound?
'Tis pity, my brethren, you're all consigned
To the rule of a man with a narrow mind!"
This said, to the cloister he hied away,
To chafe and to fret—but not to pray.

III.

" I will make that lordly Abbot fear ;
He shall hear again of this !"
But the Abbot was singing the Vespers clear,
And did never the novice miss
Till night ; when his toils and cares were done,
And he counted his children one by one.
" How fares with our novice, good Brother John ?
Does he take to our rule of life ?"
" Dear Father, his will is very strong,
And, fresh from a world of strife,
He suffers no contradiction yet ;
He cannot his ancient state forget."
"'Tis sad ; yet, my brother, his failings bear ;
Remember, we all are weak :
Let his horse and his hound have the best of care ;
To gain him by kindness seek :
'Twill be on our Order a grievous blot
If the power of holiness touch him not !"
" Father, I fear we shall lose him." "Son.
'Tis by love and by prayer that souls are won."

"Father, your blessing," his head he bent,
It was given: then each to his slumber went.
And the Abbot rose 'ere the dawn of day
For the soul of the restless Knight to pray.

IV.

The morning dawned—the woods were still:
As the night her shades withdrew,
Like a silver gauze o'er the heath-clad hill
Lay the bright and sparkling dew.
The Abbot prayed in the Church alone
The soul of the Knight to win;
Till over each fretted and sculptured stone,
Which in darkness long had been,
Came gleams from the eastern window pane,
Rich with many a gorgeous stain:
And in burnished glory shone
Those flowered mazes, more fair than thought,
Which the skill of the sculptor had fondly wrought.
And the Abbot was glad, for it seemed to show
How stony hearts may in Heaven's light glow,

Which we in our unbelief despise,
And the beauty of holiness o'er them rise.
Then came the solemn and soothing tone
Of the deep-mouthed Convent bell;
And, one by one, stole the brethren in,
And down on their knees they fell;
And all for a moment was hushed again
Till the echoes died away,
And up-soared in the air the exulting strain
That blesses the coming day:
Three hundred voices are singing 'Prime!'
And the Knight, is he with them there?
Alas! he stays in his cell all the time;
The seasons of praise and prayer,
He dares not their sacred call obey:
He is weary and sick, and he cannot pray.

V.

At length in these words his plaint he made:
"Good brother John, I would ask your aid,
And your counsel; my heart is sad:

Of old when the Abbey bells did ring,

I loved the Mattins and Prime to sing ;

Now, nothing can make me glad :

My body is sick, and so is my mind :

My feelings are very drear !"

" Dear Knight, I am pained," said the brother kind,

" I sometimes begin to fear

That an active life under less control,

Far better would suit both your body and soul :

Shall I go to the Abbot and state your case ?"

" Nay, brother, you argue wrong ;

It is not my life that is out of place ;

I should do very well 'ere long

If *more sympathy* were to my feelings shown :

Your proud Abbot leaves me too much alone.

Three whole days have I looked in vain

For the smallest notice ;—but stay,

I see you are vexed, so I won't complain ;

Yet the Abbot should hear what I say :

That if he will not at times unbend

He may throw back one who may stand his friend."

"Dear Knight, the Abbot gets little rest;
By many and weighty cares,
And work of all kinds, he is sore opprest;
But we all have his love, and his prayers.
And now, I bethink me, he bid me say
He rides to the Manor of Chale to day, [1]
And he asks your company by the way."
" 'Tis well," said the Knight in reply, " I had deemed
That he meant me a slight: for so it seemed."
" Dear Knight, we read in the sacred Book
That appearances oft deceive: [2]
We should not alone on the outside look,
But ever the best believe.
Did you know how three hundred imperfect men
Can respect and love him, O, doubtless, then
You would see how deep 'neath the surface lies
That life which he makes a sacrifice."
The Knight was silent: at last he said,
" If your words are true, brother John,

---

[1] The mill at Chale, and the meadows round it, belonged to the Abbey.   [2] S. John vii. 24.

These three long days, though my heart has bled,
I have done the good Abbot wrong.
I see I gave way to the moment's whim,
And cared for myself, while I misjudged him."
" Dear Knight, it is blessèd our faults to own.
But listen : the bell, with its silver tone,
Calls us."   Thus saying, they went their way :
But the novice was far too sad to pray.

VI.

The good steed neigheth beside the gate,
And prances in very pride ;
The good steed pricketh his velvet ears
For joy that his master's voice he hears.
The Abbot his mule doth ride :
Then the party start without any state,
The Abbot and Knight before,
Brother John, and another monk, behind ;
Right through the Coppice, and down the moor
And where the brooklet doth wind :
And the bloodhound bays as he bounds along,

And plunges the fens and reeds among.
Oh the summer air, it is soft and free !
And sports o'er the face like an infant's smile :
And the sweet birds are singing cheerily,
And their song doth the hour beguile :
And the lessons of nature are lessons of grace,
Where in faithful hearts they can find a place.
The Abbot at first he little said,
Perchance he did think, or pray,
But when they came to the river-bed,
He stopped to inquire the way.
Then he asked of the Knight if his steed looked well,
And smoothed down his arching crest,
And his manner was that of such perfect rest
That the Knight felt under a spell :
And as they rode soberly side by side,
Deep in his heart, but not exprest,
Was the grief and remorse that filled his breast
At his foolish charge of pride.
Yet he could not resist a passing thought :—
" These kind of men, so averse to strife,

Are only fit for the cloister life.
I should very much like to put him astride
On Grey Sultan—I don't much think he can ride ;
We should have some excellent sport.
There are some that for fight and for tournament
Are formed ; 'tis a fate their nature meant ;
And some, like our Abbot, for books and cell :
Any looker on could this lesson spell.
First example ; myself and my noble grey :
No wonder I find it dull to pray."

VII.

The river ran deep, the river ran strong,
And the ford it was far away ;
Said the Knight, " with your leave I'll go gently along
While you on the bank do stay.
If I cross unharmed you can mend your pace,
And follow when I have passed ;
If I fail, we must go to another place
Where the stream sweeps not on so fast."
" Agreed," said the Abbot, " but be not rash ;

Let my words of warning tell."
Scarce had he said when they heard a splash,
As the steed in the torrent fell,
Through catching his hoof in a rocky ledge
Just as he stept from the river's edge.
Help was in vain for man or horse :
You could barely their pathway trace
As down with the current's rushing force
They drifted with rapid pace.
At length, where a tree o'er the stream had bent,
The course of the Knight was staid ;
But not till his breath was well-nigh spent,
And his forehead a gash displayed.
The good Abbot lifted the Knight on land,
The horse made his way to the nearest strand.
An hour sped by ; on their nags again
The party were ready to mount,
But the Knight had met with an awkward sprain
In his side ; and on this account
The Abbot proposed they should change their plan :
" Brother John, let the good Knight ride

On my gentle mule, when he feels that he can ;
And see that you keep by his side.
And if he gets faint, or is needing rest,
With the Rector of Gatcombe wait :
I will go on my errand, for time doth press ;
Already I fear I am late."
Then he turned where the Knight on the ground did
    lay,
And stooping beside him, said,
" Will you lend your horse ? where I have to stay
I will see him drest and fed."
" I *will* lend, Holy Father, with right good will ;
You will find him a little hot ;
'Tis not his mode to be calm and still ;
I beseech you provoke him not :
If your skill as a horseman you doubt at all,
You had better not mount, or you'll get a fall."
But the Abbot, though thin and spare and meek,
Little the caution did seem to need,
For his clear eye flashed, as it would bespeak
Pride and delight in the gallant steed :

And when he was up 'twas a goodly sight !
His seat in the saddle and hand on the rein
Were those of a Prince ; and the prostrate Knight
Found his conscience doing its work again ;
And I saw, as the Abbot rode away,
That he covered his eyes and tried to pray.

PART II.

Life in the Abbey.

I.

" So may we knock at heaven's door,
And strive the prize of life to win;
Continually, and evermore,
Guarded without and pure within."

Ancient Hymn.

 ALMLY and softly the days sped on,
    And many a week had passed and gone,
    While time, like the wheel of the Abbey mill,
Carried life's torrent adown it still.
Long had the Knight in the Abbey staid,
And long with the brethren knelt and prayed.
Yet his love of retirement seemed to cool,
And he did not keep to the Convent rule.
' Then wherefore stay,' you ask; would you know ?
He loved the Abbot too well to go.

Every day he saw something new,
Which showed what a holy man can do.
With the thought, "I am only a novice still,
And free as a bird to depart—if I will;"
Another his conscience did sorely rack,
"I have made my election, and dare I go back?"
And thus when he felt in the mood to leave,
His want of devotion his soul would grieve.
Not on the *life* did he lay the blame,
But on his self love, so hard to tame!
He had come to the Abbey to seek relief
From earthly cares and from human grief;
'Twas an act of self pleasing; he saw it now:
And yet, at the time, his life to vow
To the Highest, so pure a work had seemed,
'Twas humbling to find he had only dreamed.
"But the aim was a true one?" "most true, good
    Knight."
Your motives, tho' mixed, were partly right;
And this you will find, as day by day,
You humble your stubborn will, and pray

II.

O think not this good man's life was lost,
Or his mind on its troubles for ever tossed
The Abbot his service oft would need.
And send him forth on his noble steed ;
Would ever find calls for the skill and might,
And the generous aid of the sturdy Knight ;
And when wearied and worn through much employ,
As the evening onwards drew,
Would his hearty affectionate talk enjoy ;
And the brethren loved him too :
And kind brother John fixed his gentle eyes
Frequently on him in glad surprise.
And yet 'twould be more than truth if I said,
That the Knight's self-conquest was perfected
In so brief a time ; it could *not* be so ;
For evil habits like ill-weeds grow,
And they root them deeper down than vice :
Then prejudice comes the heart to cramp,
Her chill breath laden with clouds of damp,
Which form o'er the soul in crusts of ice.

Do you doubt me? Is it not mostly seen,
That the humbler virtues we count as mean?
And doth not each human spirit know,
How in danger of death, or by sin brought low,
It cannot its deepest convictions smother:
And how, when life's sunshine hath re-appeared,
The judgment has either changed or veered,
And we seem, not our better self, but another?
At such moments, in nine cases out of ten,
Our good resolutions grow out of date;
We decide, " I was weak as a woman then;
My mind was not in a healthy state!"
Our Knight proved the *one case in ten;* he might fall
But he kept a true heart in spite of all.
Still, his temper continued his greatest bane;
An example will make my meaning plain;
And put what I wish to imply in form,
Though it shews the poor Knight in a terrible storm.

III.

The Abbot had sent him to Haven-street;
He could not the matter in hand complete

To return for the mid-day meal; he *did* try,
But when he got back to Quarr
The hour of refection had long gone by ;
He was hungry and cold, and he saw
That most of the brethren had left the hall;
While no one appeared to heed his call.
He rushed to the kitchen : the cook away,
The Infirmarer's place was keeping ;
The latter had watched till break of day
With a poor sick monk, and was sleeping :
Only old Peter sat there with the dog,
As deaf as a post, and as still as a log.
" Will *no* one hear? 'tis too bad," he said,
" They might have considered my toil ;
I am worked like a cart-horse, and can't get fed ;
I am *not* out of temper-- but hard bestead ;
Hot? my blood is too chilly to boil !"
Such a noise he made, such a roaring and din,
That all the lay brethren came hurrying in.
Then he vowed that he would not a day remain
In the Abbey, where even a saint must complain !

He would leave it, and tell men why: who'd prevent
    him?
Just then brother David came running apace,
And begged he'd be calm, with a piteous face,
And his dinner should quickly be sent him.
"Calm?" and he stamped again on the floor,
As his voice crescendoed almost to a roar.
"I *am* calm,—mind your business—take care not to
    venture
Your betters to bid whom you ought to obey;
For I *may* shew my teeth! Sirrah, take down that
    trencher,
Or I'll take *yourself* down in a summary way!
You'll set up as Abbot another day, will you?—
Don't shake so, you wretched old sham, I won't kill
    you!"
He turned on his heel, and the Abbot stood there;
His fine brow contracted, and saddened his air!
"My son, this *is* sorrow indeed; and I fear,
That, however it grieves you, my duty is clear.
You must go to your cell for a season." "Good Father,

I don't mind that penance, I'd very much rather."
" My son add not thus to my pain; you were tempted :
I can feel for you ; mine in a measure the blame :
I could wish you from all inconvenience exempted,
But we never should shun either censure or shame,
If our conscience upbraid : these are small ills to take,
When the Saviour of men bore so much for our sake."
Here the good Abbot paused, for the Knight looked
    distressed ;
Conviction, at last, had awoke in his breast.
" Take heart, my dear son, and from fretting refrain ;
You never may so fail in trial again !
As far as I can, your privation I'll share ;
We both have much need of contrition and prayer."
" O Father, your gentleness cuts to my soul ;
Will you pray its besetting disease be made whole ?
Were you always at hand, I could never forget."
" My son, One far nigher will succour you yet.
His pardon implore : contrite love hath prevailed,
Where pride and self-confident boasting have failed,
His compassions are deep as their compass is wide ;

O'er the poor stranded soul they flow in like a tide.
Remain in your cell till the close of the day,
And if then you would seek me you well know the
    way :
Meanwhile, don't despond or feel cheerless, but pray."

IV.

The Church in those bygone ages taught
We should make amends for wrong ;
Or done in malice, or done in sport,
To the culprit it would belong,
Not only an empty pardon to ask,
But to do for his brother some humbling task.
He had sinned against order and love, made confusion,
And his grief should be real, no mere self-delusion.
So when his incarceration had ended,
And the novice was reconciled—
For they *did* shut up full-grown men who offended,
As we shut up a half-grown child—
The Knight was reduced to friend David's department,
And went where the "wretched old sham" and his
    cart went.

" What ! a man of his rank in a menial place !"

I think I hear some exclaim,

" I can't stand *that*, 'tis a foul disgrace : "

But 'tis surely the greater shame

When one who has entered a sacred calling

Can disgrace his profession by stamping and brawling.

You think, and *I* think, it thus will remain ;

Who argue, revert to their own views again.

It so chanced that our Knight in his hearty contrition

Really grew quite at home with his humble position ;

And so zealously took to old David and carting,

That both felt distressed when the time came for
    parting.

Oft o'er the breezy hills they were wending,

What time the orb of day was ascending

In golden sheen :

Or they lingered late in the copse-wood, chopping,

Heaving the cumbrous log, or stopping

To rest between.

But whatever their way or their work might be,

They grew towards each other in sympathy.

If cramped was the old man's mental state—
And he'd puzzle and twist his words about
Before he could get his expressions out—
His gentleness gave their meaning weight :
And a look there was in his honest face
Which lent what he said a nameless grace :
A singleness, too, of heart and aim,
That frequently put the brave Knight to shame,
And taught him, not to contemn, but prize
The meekness he once could criticize.
David's conduct, moreover, seemed truly grand
To one who its spring could understand.
He would do what he *did* do with all his might,
And could not be swerved from his sense of right ;
Stop the pleasantest task when the time came for
      praying,
His whole soul absorbed in the 'hour' he was saying :
And yet, when they finished their daily employment,
He was fresh as a boy in his mirth and enjoyment.
Thus, in life, how oft we the lesson read,
That the simple peasant or child will lead

The fiery spirit naught else can rule ;
Which starts from the yoke of a sterner school :
Strange that the feeble the strong should sway !
O law of a Providence ill understood ;
Which makes e'en our weaknesses work out our good,
If only we cleave to truth's perfect way,
And long for the temper for which we pray !

PART III.

𝕿𝖍𝖊 𝕬𝖇𝖇𝖊𝖞 𝕴𝖓𝖛𝖆𝖉𝖊𝖉.

I.

" Faint not, and fret not, for threatened woe,
Watchman on truth's great height !
Few though the faithful, and fierce though the foe,
Weakness is aye Heaven's might."

Lyra Apostolica.

 SAID that the year was stealing by,
And now the snow on the woods did lie.
The oaks of Quarr were a goodly sight,
As they reared their heads in the morning light,
Massive, and rugged, and gnarled, and white !
With their antlered crests and their spreading boughs,
And their huge and upright boles ;
Beneath them the Abbey cattle browse :
Hark ! as the clock-bell tolls,
Dreamily telling the passing hour,

The Mistaken Calling.

You may chance to see something strange :
How the creatures start and assemble as one,
And then together go off at a run,
For the call to prayer from the heavy tower,
It is feeding time at the grange !
The cattle are gathered, and calmly wait
To pass the yard by the forest gate ;
With pendent heads and attentive ears :
They pause till a quiet monk appears,
Just as the bell goes down ;
And the men of the farm draw round in a ring,
And the " Angelus " strongly and sweetly sing : (¹)
While far towards the busy town,
With the moan and the wave, and the voice of the rill
The sound is wafted when winds are still.
A " Credo " and " Pater " the service end : (²)
Then the hinds and the shepherds the cattle tend.
Morning, and noon, and eve, and night,
When the shadows fall, with the dawn's grey light.
By souls through this simple method trained
May the truest object of life be gained.

Mark me, I do not mean to say
All other teaching was cast aside;
But only that each returning day
Was by devotion sanctified.
Briefly the Abbey bell suspended
The ploughman's toil on the distant hill,
And as in prayer his head he bended,
The patient ox at his side stood still:
No work so urgent, no time so prest,
That the Giver of Life remained unblest!
And we? in our more enlightened day,
Are full of good deeds,—but neglect to pray.

II

To our Knight we turn: he had drawn a seat
Near to the fire to warm his feet,
And was busily piling the glowing logs
In the form of an arch o'er the iron dogs;
When from his side his sleeping hound
Uprose with a start, and loudly bayed;
And there fell on the ear a tramping sound,

And some of the brethren were sore afraid;
But the Knight looked pleased, and his glance grew
    bright
As the eagle's, that eyes the coming fight.
Then the clanging bell an arrival told :—
'Twas a trying thing for the monks of old,
When a mounted band, without warning or word,
Came down on the brethren for bed and board.
Let this be as it might : the Abbot of Quarr,
So loved that his simple word was law,
Not for an instant surprise displayed,
No sign of offence or annoyance made :
But received his guests with a quiet grace,
Giving orders to find for all comers place.
Would you learn who he had to entertain ?
A noble widow and all her train.
The " Lady," the title by which she was known, (3)
O'er the whole of the Island she rule did bear ;
At her Courts she sat on a royal throne,
The great in the earldom her homagers were,
Save those, not a few, who their titles draw,

And hold their fiefs of the Abbot of Quarr.
You may fancy all was bustle and fuss
In an ancient community so surprised ;
By no means ; they did not manage thus
In days when religious calm was prized,
Remember the Abbot's resources vast,
And the many brethren who lived at Quarr ;
What he did, was chiefly his mind to cast
On the Monks whom he thought most fitted for
The task of contriving to meet the need
Of the numerous class he must house and feed.
The "Lady" was led to a chamber of state
Reserved for visitors, near to the gate ;
Through the Abbot's own room, approached by a
     stair.
His room, and two others, were placed at her will :
Brother John and his Monks of her comfort had care ;
The guards and attendants the corridors fill :
Over these the Knight was called to preside,
And see that their wants were well supplied.
And Martin, the cellarer, went to arrange

For the horses and men to be lodged at the Grange.
Then the Abbot a Chapter of monks eleven (¹)
Summoned to meet at the hour of seven,
After Vespers; for sadly his heart forbode
This visit no good to the Convent shewed.
All done, to the Church he went away
To chasten his anxious heart—and pray.

III.

The Chapter met their affairs to discuss :
And each one sat in his stall
While the Abbot opened the business thus,
As a matter concerning them all.
" You know how since among you I came,
My teaching has ever been the same :
To overcome hatred by love, and be
Through meekness known in adversity.
Not to struggle, nor strive, when life's billows rave,
But to rise by faith o'er their foaming crest ;
Well knowing that they who thus mount the wave,
Are carried unscathed to a certain rest.

Yet haply a higher law controls,
And those whom the Holy One hath given
A charge involving the cure of souls,
To a stronger course are, reluctant, driven ;
May be called to wage, if in trust for Him,
What may seem to the world like a carnal fight.
But 'tis time to make ending of metaphors dim :
Know, the Lady of Fortibus claims the right
To appoint to our churches : but I can shew
By our founder's law it was never so :
When Father Jordan and Father Paul
Go hence to Palestine,
Brading and Godshill will vacant fall :—
And Father Ambrose has had a call
To a parish a hundred miles away,
And will Kingston soon resign.
And dear Father Christopher dying lies—
Even now he may rest in Paradise !
" The Lady" announces that Canon Gray,
Her kinsman, shall be to Brading ordained ;
And a Sherborne priest has her promise gained

For Kingston and Yaverland.—Well-a-day
For the hapless flock, if the shepherds stray
Already his livings are forty-three!　(5)
And he farms them out to unworthy men!
If she her unholy will obtain,
Vainly to us will our churls complain:　(6)
No relief can we give them then!
I cannot my way through these troubles see.
Quarr Charter, I told her, expressly said,
The livings were all in the gift of its head.　(7)
But no! she looked angry, and did not choose
To acknowledge the rights I so strongly urged;
And if she appeal to the Crown, we lose,
And our peaceful island in strife is merged.
Alas! my brethren, we all shall need
Patience and faith, for our hearts must bleed!"
Sadly the brethren their Abbot heard;
And as evening wore along,
Many a wise and solemn word
Was uttered by many a tongue:
Tho' opinions differed as to the way

They must meet the coming snare;
But all were agreed to fast and pray,—
For the staff of the monk is prayer.
While pensively thus the monks conversed,
The Knight, by the Abbot's leave,
Sat behind the stalls, so he knew the worst;
And deeply his heart did grieve.
And he thought, "O what would I give to close
In mortal fight with the Abbot's foes!"
You fight them, my friend, in the truest way,
When you learn to subdue yourself, and pray.

IV.

Wait we awhile by the Abbot's couch,
When night had closed around him;
He bends to kneel, but doth rather crouch;
And thus that brother found him
Whose name sweetly on memory falls,
The "beloved disciple" its sound recals.
Right worthy "John" that name to bear,
Endowed with riches and graces rare.

The Mistaken Calling.

Ever he copied its pattern high,
Dwelling in love unceasingly.
But e'en love like his could not now remove
The anguish that One alone could soothe.
Still, while the tender brother knelt
Long at his side, the mourner felt
Such love was the earnest left him yet
Of a Higher that cannot sleep, forget !
Wakefully passed the weary night ;
Clearly before the Abbot's sight
The future outspread he saw,
(Or seemed to see, as in a glass
O'er which successive objects pass :)
Some of the brethren, well he knew,
Would chafe at his strong unbending view,
Wish to change their ancient law,
To yield to the " Lady's" haughty " fiat"
All that she asked for the sake of quiet.
So disaffection might make its way,
Creeping in silence on,
Till the peace of the Abbey became its prey ;

And united feeling gone,
The monks, by timidity urged and led,
Might begin to wish for another head.
Some ambitious spirit would thus find scope
For a scarce-acknowledged but cherished hope,
As yet but seen in the distance dim,
That their reverend Father, if forced to yield,
Would resign the struggle and quit the field,
And the choice of the brethren fall on him !
Did he really know what his monks would do ?
We need not to such a conclusion leap :
He only those in his guidance knew
As a careful shepherd knows his sheep.
Not that sheep I compare to the human race,
Men are far more wise and less innocent ;
But they say that each sheep has a different face !
You will find it if on the search intent.
Just so an experienced ruler knows
Those who in trouble would prove his foes ;
For a Convent is but a minor realm,
A little world in a narrow sphere ;

And the master spirit who guides the helm
Sees that his power would disappear,
(In spite of laws in which all agreed,)
If its 'prestige' failed him in time of need——
Through the working of either a secret faction,
Or his failure in any great transaction.
What made the Abbot's prospects lower,
And seem more in gloom from hour to hour,
Was this:—To *most* of the brethren dear,
One in the Abbey he well might fear.
Sub-Prior of a house not far from thence,
He left in disgrace, I will not tell why;
Was received through the Abbot's benevolence,
But worked him evil continually.
The Abbot in fact had known for long
That much in his fold was going wrong,
Through this man's efforts a feud to raise,
Where all should be love and prayer and praise.
Can we wonder he watched till break of day,
Looking in faith for the living ray
That gilds the sorrows of those who pray.

PART IV.

The Return Home.

I.

"And peace, for war is needless,
   And rest, for storm is past,
And goal from finished labour,
   And anchorage at last."

N silence the noble Abbey lies,
   Till the dawn of returning day
   Draws the sunbeam down from the glow-
      ing skies,
To kiss the dew away;
While the hare sits on the sparkling lawn,
Side by side with the Abbot's fawn:
That fawn, the gift of a little child,
Plaything, or ward, alternate styled;
An orphan, left in the world alone,
Whom the gentle Abbot had made his own.

The Mistaken Calling.

He was fairly dowered, that orphan child!
And, in virtue of wardship, the Abbot mild
Might his rental claim till he came of age : (*)
But a higher ambition his thoughts engage.
The little one he would train to know
The God who protected his childish years ;
On the rental he did not a thought bestow :
It was all laid by, and he had no fears
That the noble boy would his wealth misspend,
Whom he taught to make the poor man his friend.
But the time goes on, I must tell my tale :
And see ! all assembled around the gate,
An array of Knights, till a lady pale
Mounts her white steed as the clock tolls eight,
And departs on her way.   But who doth ride
On that war-horse, unmatched in form, by her side ?
'Tis the Knight! who has said a long farewell
To'Quarr Abbey ; and hurries back
In his Norman Keep once more to dwell :
Sorely his heart will lack
The loving converse so long enjoyed ;

Nor fail to experience an aching void.
" For his duty," his friend the Abbot said,
" Was to live with his vassals, and be their head.
It was work for Heaven, and Heaven's work was blest ;
In later years he might look for rest ;
And from time to time, might his struggling will
Humble in prayer in their cloister still."
But plainly the Abbot before him set,
He had not a monk's vocation yet.
" He had kept him," he said, " for many a day,
For his soul's health received his vow ;
For they only can rule who have learned to obey :
But he earnestly charged him now
Not to go thence, and his true aim bide,
By giving way to his nature's pride.
But to show that religion can be of use
To the warrior, as well as the calm recluse."
The lady of Fortibus tried to seek,
As they ambled to Carisbrooke,
For the good Knight's thoughts of the Abbot meek ;
He could scarcely her manner brook,

Till it came in his mind he might help the right,
By putting resentment out of sight.
So he talked of the Abbot's gentle rule,
Of his work with such patience done ;
Of the ardour that never seemed to cool,
If ought might for heaven be won ;
Of the love that he bore him : he faltered here,
And let fall on his charger's neck a tear !
" The Lady" was struck, as she well might be,
The sturdy soldier so moved to see !
But her speech she resumed : " Her opinion ran,
[She feared she was giving pain,]
That the Abbot must be an ambitious man,
And full of the love of gain.
Why else does he grasp at the livings all
That vacant within my earldom fall ?"
I need not stay to describe the rest
Of the converse ; suffice, that the Knight was prest ;
But he kept his temper, and held his own,
Till "the Lady" spoke in a softened tone.
" Good Knight," she exclaimed at last, " I was wrong

To promise those livings; I would recal,
If I might, my steps; but my promise has long
Been given : the preferment soon will fall.
Can you tell me how I can ease my mind,
And a better mode of arranging find ?"
He paused for a moment, then spake again :
" My offer a thousand marks ensures,
An' it please you, to both the reverend men
To whom you assigned the Abbot's cures :
This amount will well reimburse your friends,
And for all disappointment make amends.
I can spare the money; I only need
For payment to know that my plans succeed.
" The Lady" was silent, and almost shamed ;
But the Knight had her haughty feelings tamed.
In spite of her wealth, she the gift could deign
To take, and her claim withdraw ;
For herself and her heirs, she would henceforth refrain
From presenting the livings of Quarr. (⁹)
How the heart of the good Knight leaped that day
As he bent o'er his horse's mane to pray !

II.

The Norman Castle to sounds of mirth
Re-echoed : from vale and hill
At the Knight's return come his vassals forth,
And its ample courtyard fill.
And long on his accents with joy they hung ;
For the boy he had made his heir was young,
And seldom among them came.
And the time, how heavily it had passed !
Unmarked and unmeasured by feast and fast,
It was ever one dreary same.
But now the hours go merrily round,
For each tenant his master and chief has found.
Did this chief his duties neglect or slight ?
Was he less on good deeds intent ?
Less bold in the saddle, less brave in the fight,
Than when to the Abbey he went ?
No ! his heart that of yore for its *own* sorrow bled,
Now the sorrows of all would share ;
Wherever occasion his footsteps led,
The grieved and oppressed were his care :

And all who roam homeless the land about,
The Knight or his chaplain would find them out.
" The Chaplain ?" no matter from whence he came,
But " good Brother John" was his usual name!
And through many a season, day by day,
" Brother John" and the Knight together pray.

III.

They pray and they work : they do their parts
With patient faith and unswerving hearts.
The same kind of trial the Knight befals
Which vexed his soul in the Abbey walls ;
But temptation baffled soon loses force,
Till it comes to be met as a thing of course.
Then we learn that the cares of life fulfil
The work of Heaven on the chastened will :
That the rugged heart in its pride and might
Needs the sharp file of suffering to keep it bright.
And if all in this world that we highest prize
Must be compassed by stern self-sacrifice ;
The merchant's wealth, the mechanic's fame,

The statesman's ambition, the student's aim
Not to mention love, which doth know no rest,
Till through long-tried constancy truly blest :
What wonder the glories that faith can trace
Must bo won—as a runner wins a race !
True, the runner's strength he may scarce control,
But he trains his body, and girds his soul ;
And but gains the reward of his toil at last,
When the fight is o'er and the struggle past.
"So the doctrine of works you mean to preach !"—
Dear reader you should not chide,
I do but quote what the Scriptures teach,
And add not a word beside. ([10])
"Well ! morals I hate : they lead one a dance !"
I stand rebuked ; and will only glance
At one more fact in the Knight's career.
You may see him his Norman fortress near :
Fair is the sight to the gazer's eye,
As it shews in the grandeur of bastion and keep,
Terraced high on the grassy steep,
Boldly against the glowing sky.

Doth he realize that the whole was given
To his heir, when he gave himself to Heaven?
He does: at his monarch's strong behest
Its charge he will still retain,
But he walks its halls as a passing guest,
Nor calls it his own again:
Save the holy precincts where rest awhile
His gentle bride in her early grave:
She whose sweet presence, whose gladdening smile
Fell soft as the oil on the troubled wave.
Madly he loved her, with all the power
Of his own strong nature; but, like a flower
That shows no symptom of quick decay,
She was only lent for a passing day.
No one the cause of her illness knew;
More gentle, and loving, and still, she grew;
More closely around his heart she twined,
As her spirits drooped and her health declined:
Remedies reached not her weakened state,
They were wrongly chosen, or came too late.
One short summer and she was gone!

The poor Knight's anguish was deep and long,
But the trial of lengthened suffering
No blessing seemed to his soul to bring.
He indulged in a bitter, resentful mood,
(As one who is under Heaven's ban,)
To his vassals and all the neighbourhood;
And lived a lonely and morbid man,
Both with the world and himself at war—
You know the rest, how he came to Quarr,
Dreaming his grief might pass away,
If his mind could rest, and his heart could pray.

IV.

He *dreamed:* but it is not delusion now
That brightens his eye and calms his brow.
We left him just when he turned to gaze
On his fair demesne; while the air tint's haze
Fell like the earnest of peace and love
O'er his distant future lying.
Mark him: his eyes are fixed above,
The resemblance in thought applying:

And doubt not the same deep holy calm,
Shall the present of life console, embalm.
But the King his services needs ; to quell
A raid of the Welsh : he must once more dwell
In a noisy camp, and his life resign
To the fortune of war, or to Love Divine !
That fortune how blest, and that Love how near,
When he falls transfixed by a foeman's spear :
For his spirit, by earthly toils is prest,
And longs to escape to its heavenly rest.
He has swooned ; and his life-blood ebbs away ;
They would bear him back to his castle grey.
But no : he opens his languid eye,
And looks at his friends beseechingly.
He fain would speak 'ere they rise to go,
But his thoughts half wander, his voice is low.
" Take me to Quarr ;" he cries, " I would be
On the peaceful shore of the Solent sea.
Take me to Quarr ; I would hear the chime
Of the Abbey bells, at the hour of " Prime."
My soul is athirst for the strains of praise

The Mistaken Calling.

The brethren in choir so sweetly raise,
Take me to Quarr; I would lay my head
In my quiet cell: on the pallet bed
Where of yore, like a tired child, I slept,
While the moonlight across the water crept.
Take me to Quarr: for my soul doth sigh
For the Abbot's blessing 'ere I die!"
His desire is granted; the way seems long,
But the tide of life in its ebb grows strong,
And lasts till his resting place is won.
And " Bless thee, my true, my noble son,"
Is the greeting that falls on his dying ear
From the holy lips of the Abbot dear.
They must lose no time, for his hour is nigh,
The Abbot removes the standers by,
And stays awhile with the Knight alone :
The last good Food was softly given ;
And 'ere a calm half hour had flown,
So calm, 'twas the blending of earth and Heaven
The brethren repaired to the Church to pray,
For the soul of the Knight had passed away.

Conclusion.

TO THE READER.

 MUST bid you "good bye," for my tale
is done:

One-sided, I'll not deny;

But whenever we speak of the rays of the sun,

They suggest a cloudless sky.

I admit that dark clouds o'er the faith arose,

The blindest this fact must allow;

Yet, though shrouded at times, it were wrong to
suppose

That old annals no rays of that glory disclose

Which kindles our atmosphere now.

And whatever we think, Holy Love is the same;

It leads to self-sacrifice, *passions must tame.*

'Tis the sum of perfection in all **Christian men;**

The **Cloister** gave scope for its exercise then;

And wealth lent its aid the same truth to work out ;
That the Monks were good landlords no wise man
    will doubt :
And yet through their riches they fell : it is clear,
Had their lives been more simple, they still had been
    here.
A dispassionate study of history displays
More Abbots of Quarr than our guesses would raise.
Let us own it ; nor deem we perfection have gained,
As a nation, because from excesses restrained
By our strong moral code : it *is* blessèd, I say,
For the frail and imperfect to be
So hedged by opinion, they scarcely can stray :
But in looking around we must see
That our fathers a purer ideal maintained ;
That the true marks of sanctity farther off lie :
And that if, in despite of this, wickedness reigned,
And we don't sink so low : yet we rarely rise high.

Notes.

(¹) " And the Angelus strongly and sweetly sing."

The Angelus is the Angelical Salutation : see Luke i. 28.   This is sung in religious houses at what are called the Canonical Hours, viz : nine, twelve, three, and six : nine a.m. being the hour at which our LORD was sentenced to death, and also the time of day when the HOLY GHOST descended at Pentecost ; twelve, the hour when our LORD was crucified ; three, when He gave up His Spirit into the Hands of His FATHER ; six, when He was taken down from the Cross and laid in the grave.   These hours were also " canonical," or hours of public prayer under the Jewish dispensation.   See Acts ii. 15 ; iii. 1 ; &c.

(²) " A credo and pater the service end."

From the earliest period of our national history after the introduction of Christianity, it was the custom for the farm servants to stop work when the bells of the nearest Abbey rang for the service ; at such times they were taught to say the Belief, and the Lord's Prayer, with heads uncovered.   The practice was British as well as Saxon.

An old Welsh triad of the sixth century makes allusion to it.

" Hast thou heard what Bruno sung ?
Chant thy Pater and thy Creed :
From death flight will not avail."

And again in the words of a very old Welsh poet :

" Thou didst not chant thy Pater Noster
Either at Matins or Vespers."

See Eccles : remains of the Cymry, &c.

(3) " The Lady," the title by which she was known."

The Lady here alluded to is Isabella de Fortibus, who possessed the sovereignty of the Isle of Wight in the reign of Henry III. and the earlier part of that of Edward I. Upon her death-bed, being childless, she was persuaded to make over the Earldom to the Crown. But subsequent remonstrances, raised by parties claiming the Island by descent from its ancient possessors, led to a judicial inquiry as to the kind of persuasion which had been used. Those who are conversant with the reign of Edward I. will feel tolerably sure that the decision was in favour of the Crown. It was made upon the evidence of one of the Bishops who assisted at the signing of the Will, and who asserted upon oath that she was a consenting party to the transfer. Many historians, however, are of opinion that it was an unwilling consent, forced from her by moral coercion, rather than a matter of unbiassed choice; and it must be acknowledged that the whole affair has an awkward look.

————

(4) "Then the Abbot a Chapter of monks eleven."

Monasteries were governed by Chapters, or what we should call a Council. There were small private Chapters held for occasional purposes, and larger, or general Chapters, for matters of deeper deliberation. A Council of eleven, under the Abbot, in days when symbolism prevailed as a popular form of teaching religious truths, would be looked upon as representing figuratively our Lord and His eleven faithful Apostles. The omission of Judas from the number may account for the superstitious prejudice which still prevails against any assembly of persons who number thirteen, called together for any purpose, either serious or convivial.

(⁵) " Already his livings are forty-three !"

The holding of forty-three livings at once was far from uncommon in the thirteenth century. John Mansell, a favourite of Henry III, held no less than seven hundred! The thing was managed in this way. The livings were let, or farmed out, as it was called, to certain parties, who agreed to see that the Churches were served, and the parishioners cared for. Poor Clerks, or Curates, were then put into residence on very meagre allowances : the profits of the living, above what was paid to the incumbent, went into the pocket of the factor or agent to whom it was farmed.

(⁶) " Vainly to us will our churls complain."

Churl at that period was not a term of reproach, it merely signified agriculturalist. Churl is derived from the Saxon word Ceorle, a husbandman.

(⁷) " Quarr charter, I told her, expressly said
The livings were all in the gift of its head."

It is not pretended that all these livings were in the Abbot's gift. The names are inserted at hap-hazard to fill up the narrative, exactness of detail not being necessary to its general truthfulness. I have already stated that the main features are correctly given. Great accuracy can hardly be expected when so few records are extant. That many more might be elicited by indirect research there can be little doubt, but unless the object were more immediately historical the result of such research would hardly repay the time and labour expended upon it.

(⁸) " In virtue of wardship the Abbot mild
    Might his rental claim till he came of age."

This was the usual law of wardship in that period. Wards were legitimate sources of profit, and as such were let by the Crown, or given away in remuneration of services done to the Crown. An heir had often great difficulty in recovering his own estate when entitled to its enjoyment, from the reluctance shown by his Guardian to part with such lucrative property.

(⁹) " For herself and her heirs she would henceforth refrain
    From presenting the livings of Quarr."

See her Charter to Quarr Abbey, Dugdale's Monasticon. Vol. V. (New Edition) page 319.

For the information of the curious in such matters, the following list of parishes in which the Abbey had property, or Church patronage, is appended.

Isle of Wight.

Binstead, close to the Abbey. Binstead was in all probability the Grange, which supplied the Abbey with food. The word binstead means standing place or station for corn, &c.

New Church.—The old parish Church of Ryde. Patronage and land.

Newport.—Church patronage. Fisheries, Mills, and Salt Marshes.

Carisbrooke.—Land and Presentation, up to a certain period, to the parish Church, and the titles of the Chapel of St. Nicholas within the Castle walls.

Arreton.—Church and land.

Whippingham.—Church patronage and land.

Godshill.—Church and land.

Gatecomb.—Land.

Chale, Mill, and land, and, *probably*, the charge of keeping the S. Catherine's light burning. Chale farm shews the remains of accommodation for a cell or small body of monks.

Besides the above, Quarr Abbey had property in the parishes of Shallfleet, Newtown, Ningwood, Bonchurch, S. Boniface, Compton, Calbourne, &c.

The Abbey property in England was situated in Hampshire, Dorsetshire, Somersetshire, and Devonshire.

In Hants, the following parishes are on record :— Newnham, Lymington, Sway, Christ Church, Fleet, Staplehurst, Rownams, Cosham, Barbeflete, near Portsmouth, and Milford.

In Dorset,—Wraxhall S. Mary, and Piddletown.

In Somerset,—Hardington Mandeville.

In Devonshire,—Ford and Forway.

Two other manors, those of Drayton, and Besselsleigh, I am inclined to locate in Berkshire, near Abingdon; one branch of a very important Isle of Wight family, the De Lisles, having possessed large estates in that county, and intermarrying with the family at Besselsleigh; but it must be owned that this idea is rather hypothetical, and rests upon no very sure foundation.

The Abbey of Quarr was likewise endowed with considerable property in Normandy.

([m]) 1 Cor. ix. 21.

PRINTED BY W. R. BOWDEN, HOLYWELL STREET, OXFORD.

www.ingramcontent.com/pod-product-compliance
Lightning Source LLC
Chambersburg PA
CBHW032344020726
47499CB00009B/3166